lauren child

whoOps!
But it wasn't
me

PUFFIN

Text based on script written by

Bridget Hurst and Carol Noble

Illustrations from the TV animation

produced by Tiger Aspect

PUFFIN BOOKS
Published by the Penguin Group: London, New York, Australia,
Canada, India, Ireland, New Zealand and South Africa
Penguin Books Ltd, Registered Offices: 80 Strand, London WC2R ORL, England

penguin.com

First published 2006
Published in this edition 2007
1 3 5 7 9 10 8 6 4 2

Made and printed in China
ISBN: 978-0-141-50066-9

I have this little sister Lola.
     She is small and very funny.
Sometimes Lola likes to play
          with my things.
Usually I don't mind.

One day I come home from school
 with the best thing I have ever made.

Lola says, "Ooooh!"

I say,
"It took me ten days,
    three hours and forty minutes
to make the outside,
        which is called
the superstructure...

"... It's built from

three cereal packets,

ten yoghurt pots,

28 bottle tops, 157 sweet wrappers and a roll of extra-wide tinfoil."

Lola says, "Ooooh!"

I say, "Don't touch it!
This rocket is really breakable.
I don't mind you playing with
most of my things,
but you must double,
triple promise
you'll NEVER play
with it."

"Let's **play** something
      else then," says Lola.
    I say, "I've promised to play football
      with Marv."
"But what am I going to do?" says Lola.
      And I say, "Why don't you **play**
    with Soren Lorensen?"

Soren Lorensen is Lola's imaginary friend.
No one can see him except for Lola.

And Lola says,
    "Soren Lorensen **always** wants
to **play** with me."

"Hello, Soren Lorensen," says Lola.
"Charlie's gone to play football with Marv,
so we can play a very good game,
can't we?"

And Soren Lorensen says,
          "Yes, with those two hyenas
that are brothers and twins and
    that tiny small elephant."

Lola says, "Oh yes, Ellie.

"Where will the adventure be?"

Soren Lorensen says,
"The place where all the animals live."

And Lola says,
"In Animal Land."

Soren Lorensen says, "Ellie is really **sad** because he doesn't like the nasty **hyenas** laughing at him."

"Those **hyenas** are **meanies**, aren't they?" says Lola.
"What are we going to do?"

"We can't leave Ellie all **sad**," says Lola.
"He must go back to all his nice friends in **Animal** Land...
but **how** are we going to get him there?"

Then Soren Lorensen points to the rocket.

Lola says,
"But that is an extremely breakable and special rocket
and Charlie said that we should never,
NEVER touch it or play with it."

"But I think what Charlie meant was that if
we did play with it, we must be extra
specially careful," says Soren Lorensen.

So Lola reaches up to get the rocket.

Soren Lorensen says,
    "Remember to be extra
specially careful, Lola."

And Lola says,

"I am!
  I am!"

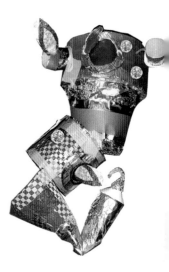

Then she says,

"Oh no!"

Lola looks at the pieces of broken rocket.
"You know, I think that when
things are broken they can always be
mended and made like new..."

"If we both act normally, Lola,
then Charlie might not think
we did it," says Soren Lorensen.

Lola whispers,
"No, he'll never know."

When I get home I shout,
"My rocket!
Lola!
Did you break
my rocket?"

Lola says,
"I didn't break your
rocket, Charlie."

I say,
"You are telling a big lie, Lola!
And you know it!"

"Don't tell Mum!"
says Lola. "Wait, Charlie!
I just have to quickly talk
to Soren Lorensen."

Lola says, "Do you think we should tell him
what really happened?"
Soren Lorensen says, "Maybe we could tell Charlie
somebody else broke the rocket?"
And Lola says, "Yes! Because it is nearly true!"

So Lola comes to talk to me.
"Charlie, Soren Lorensen and me have got something
very **extremely** important to tell you."

I say, "What?"

Lola says,
"It is the real **true** story of who **broke**
your special **rocket**.

"Well, me and Soren Lorensen were playing in our room, Charlie, and Ellie needed to go in your rocket.

I didn't think it was a good idea, but he had to get away.

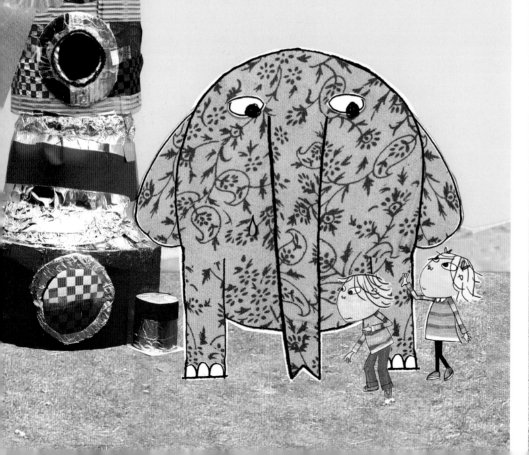

So we **squeezed**
Ellie, and it was
a real **squish**.
But we **did** it.

And then we **took off**.

Whoosh! Whoosh!

"... and then we landed 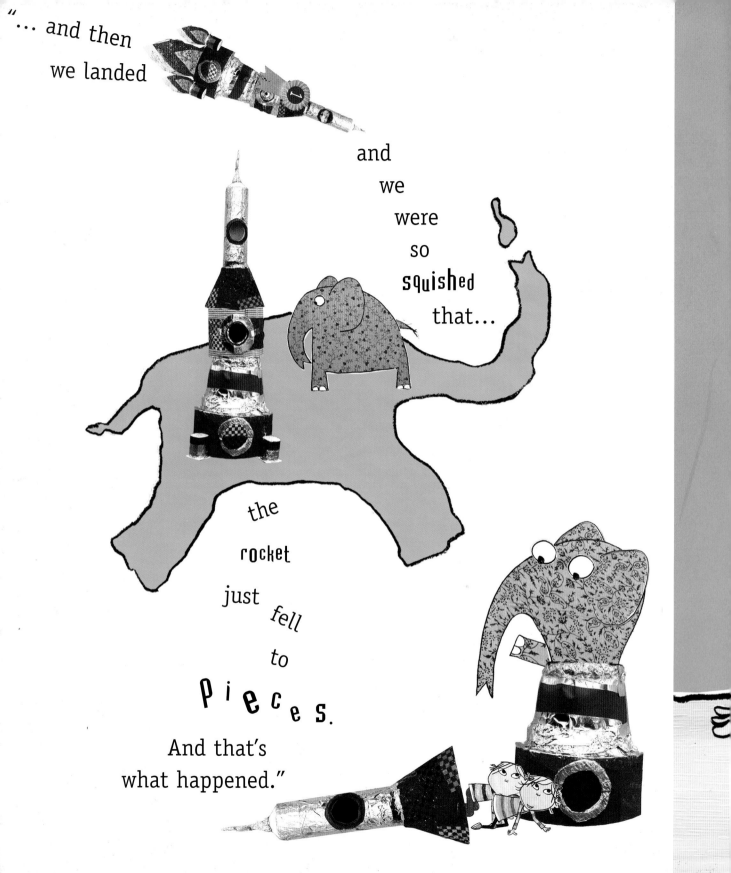 and we were so squished that...

the rocket just fell to Pieces.

And that's what happened."

I say,

"Right.
I'm going to
tell **Mum!**"

"Oh dear, I don't think he
believed us," says Soren Lorensen.

Lola says,
"I think I have to tell
    Charlie the **truth**. But will it
make Charlie **like** me again?"

Soren Lorensen says,
"As long as you say **sorry** too."

Lola knocks at the door.
"Soren Lorensen
really wants to say sorry
for breaking your
rocket, Charlie."

So I just shut
the door.

Then there's another knock
and Lola says,
"It was me that broke
your rocket. Just as I was
getting your extremely
special rocket down from
the really high shelf...
it fell and broke
into lots
of pieces.

I am really ever so sorry
for breaking your
extremely special rocket,
Charlie."

And I say,
"Are you **really**, Lola?"

Lola says, "**Sorry**, Charlie."

And she does look really very sorry.

So I say, "That's OK.
At least you've told the truth."

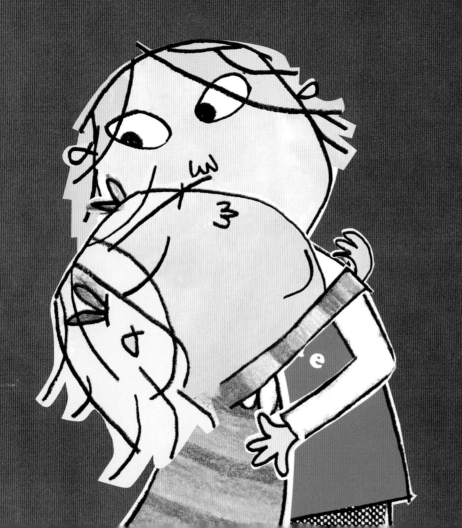

Then Lola sees the rocket.

"You **men**d**ed** it, Charlie!" she says.

And I say,
"Yes, Lola, I've **mended** it."